CHIN LING

The Chinese Cricket

CHIN LING

The Chinese Cricket

by ALISON STILWELL

THE STILWELL STUDIO - CARMEL, CALIFORNIA - 1981

For my grand-daughters,
ELISABETH and SARAH

First edition printed in United States of America
Macmillan Company, Publisher.

Second special edition for Cadmus Books
Published by E.M. Hale and Company

Third edition printed in Beijing, China
by Guoji Shudian.

Published by the Stilwell Studio,
P.O. Box 50, Carmel, California, 93921

Library of Congress Catalog Card No.: 81—90045

ISBN 0-9605862-0-2

THE STORY OF
THE CHINESE CRICKET

Not so very long ago there lived in the great country of China, just outside the walls of the old city of Beijing, a little cricket. He did not have a name, because crickets don't care about naming their children the way people do.

The little cricket lived in a big field with his mother and father and all his brothers and sisters. They would leap and hop in the tall grasses, and wrestle with one another for exercise.

The little cricket was the smallest one in all the field, and his brothers and the other crickets could easily beat him in their wrestling games. He was afraid of one of them, a big fierce-looking black cricket who always picked out the smallest cricket and beat him every time. This made him very sad because he wanted more than anything to be big and strong, and a champion wrestler.

One day he was sitting on a blade of grass, all by himself, feeling very lonesome and sad. Suddenly something large and dark came down over him, and he felt himself being lifted into the air!

He was very frightened. He began to hop around to look for a way out; then he felt himself falling and sliding, out into the sunlight again. But now he was inside a large basket with lots and lots of other crickets.

·He could not imagine what had happened. He turned to the cricket beside him, a pale one with a lame leg, to ask where they were.

"We have been captured," said the lame cricket. "They will take us to the market place in the city and sell us. People will buy the strongest ones to fight in the cricket ring."

"But what will happen to crickets like you and me?" asked the little cricket. "You are lame and I am so small."

"I am afraid that we who are weak will never be sold. We will probably be thrown out in a field to find our way home as best we can. I know, because that is what happened to an uncle of mine."

At that moment the basket was swung up from the ground, and the little cricket knew they were on their way to the great market inside the walls of Beijing. With a sinking heart he settled himself down to wait as patiently as he could.

Soon they came to a great open space where hundreds of people were walking about, talking and waving their arms.

The man who was carrying the crickets set his baskets down with a thud, and began to set up his little shop. First he spread a blue cloth on top of a table, and then he arranged on it several cages and jars. Then he separated the big strong crickets from the little weak ones, putting the big ones on top of the table where they could be seen. The little cricket was left in the basket with the weak ones and they were placed under the table. They were very worried and wondered what would happen next.

Soon a large man came up to the little shop. He pulled out a handkerchief to mop his face, as it was a warm day, and even took off his little round black hat to mop his head, which was bald.

He pointed to a large cricket and asked, "What is the price of that one?"

The shopkeeper answered, "This fine big cricket? He is sure to be a great champion in the cricket ring, but I will let you have him for only two dollars."

"What?" cried the fat man. "Why, that's ridiculous! This cricket looks thin and weak to me. He isn't worth forty cents, I am sure. However, I will offer you sixty-five cents for him."

All this talk sounded very strange to the little cricket, and he asked his new friend what was happening.

"They are bargaining," the lame cricket answered. "The shopkeeper tries to sell us for as much money as possible, and the people try to pay as little as they can."

"Oh, I see," said the little cricket, nodding his head, and he again began to listen to the two men.

The fat man had just offered a dollar for the big cricket and was about to walk away when the shopkeeper suddenly called, "All right, he is yours for a dollar!"

So the big cricket was put into a cage and the fat man took him away.

Many other people came and bought crickets at the shop until all of the big strong ones were gone and only the little ones were left.

A nice-looking lady came by and bought the lame cricket, which made him very happy. The little cricket was happy too, as he could see his friend would have a good home.

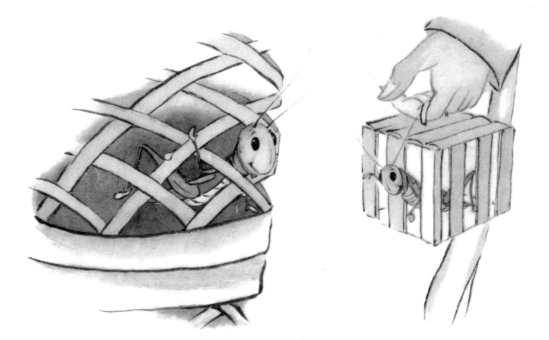

The shopkeeper stretched his arms and said to himself, "I have done a good business today. I think I will close up the shop. These weak ones will never sell, so I may as well put them out in a field somewhere."

Just then a little boy of about seven or eight came slowly up to the shop and stood looking at the remaining crickets with an anxious expression. He was dressed in faded but very clean blue coat and trousers, black shoes, and white socks. His head was shaved except for two locks of hair at either side, which were tied with red yarn. In his hand he clutched three pennies; and his bright black eyes were fastened on our friend, the little cricket! The cricket decided right away that he liked this little boy.

The boy turned to the shopkeeper and asked, "How much is this one?"

And the man replied, "This fine cricket? He is worth at least ten pennies, but you may have him for five."

"I will give you two pennies for him and one penny for a cage to put him in," said the little boy, who knew how to bargain as well as any grownup.

He wanted the little cricket more than anything in the world and had saved all his money to buy one, but he pretended that he did not really want him at all.

The shopkeeper did not even try to get a higher price.

He just said, "Well, I am in a hurry to close up now; so you can have both the cricket and a cage for the three pennies. But just as a favor, you understand."

He picked up the little cricket and, placing him in a small bamboo cage, handed him over to the little boy, who solemnly paid the money.

As the little boy walked down the street, he lifted the cage so he could look into it and said, "Hello, little cricket! Do not be afraid of me. I will take good care of you and feed you well so that you will grow fat and strong."

The little cricket was so excited and happy at finding such a good master that he hopped around and started to sing as if he would never stop. He did not stop even when his wings were tired (for that is how crickets sing, you know) and the little boy walked along, listening with a pleased smile on his face.

Soon they came to a small house near the city wall. Some children were playing blindman's buff in the little street. They stopped when they saw the little boy, and ran over to see his cricket. After they had all looked in the cage, the little boy went on down the street toward his house.

Turning in at a little red gate, he called, "Mother, I am home again!"

At his call his mother came to the doorway of their shabby little house and said, "That is good, Little Mushroom. Your supper is almost ready."

Now the little boy's name was really Guo Zhu, which means Pillar of the Country and is a very honorable Chinese name. But his mother called him Little Mushroom as a nickname, because he wasn't much bigger than one!

Little Mushroom was a very good son, so he hurried to help his mother prepare their supper. But first he set the cricket's cage down on the window sill.

The little cricket watched them eat their simple meal of noodles and a few vegetables, and decided they must be very poor. The house had only one room, and its two windows were covered with paper instead of glass. It had a small charcoal stove and a kang in one corner.

A kang is a Chinese bed. It is made of bricks and has a stove inside to keep it warm in wintertime. This one had two quilts folded up on it, one red and one blue, and there were two square pillows at the end.

When they had finished eating and had washed their bowls, the little boy brought his cricket over to show his mother.

She smiled and said, "This is a very fine one. It is said they bring good luck."

Little Mushroom knew that his mother could not find work, and they did not have much money left to buy food; so he wished with all his heart that his cricket *would* bring them luck.

"Do not worry too much, Mother," he said. "We will get along somehow."

Suddenly he gave a start and cried, "Why, I have forgotten *your* supper, little cricket! Would you like something to eat?"

The cricket was very pleased to hear this; for, to tell the truth, he *had* been feeling a bit empty. He watched Little Mushroom bring over a tiny dish with some Hairy Bean mashed up in it. And when he took his first bite he thought he had never tasted anything so good.

After he had finished he sang awhile, which was his way of saying "Thank you." Both Little Mushroom and his mother were very pleased.

After the little boy had gone to bed that night and his mother sat sewing by the table, Little Mushroom sat straight up and cried, "Mother! I have not given my cricket a name! What would be a good name for him?"

The little cricket was so excited he could hardly keep still. He was to have a name, just like a person!

The room was quiet as they all thought, and then the mother, Mrs. Liu, said, "He should have an official name, and then a nickname too, don't you think? You might call him Fu, which means good luck."

"Oh yes, Mother," cried Little Mushroom. "That would be a perfect name! But what could we call him as a nickname?"

"Well now, let me see," said Mrs. Liu as she thought hard.

Little Mushroom thought too, and then he said, "He sings as beautifully as the Golden Bell crickets, the ones called Chin Ling. Could we name him that?"

"I think we could, Little Mushroom," said his mother. "And I think it is just right for him."

So that is what he was called ever afterward.

As the days went by, Chin Ling grew fatter and stronger. Little Mushroom fed him the Hairy Bean and took him for walks in his cage so he would have lots of fresh air and sunshine.

One day Mrs. Liu made the little cricket a tiny hat with a red button on the top. He would wear it very proudly whenever he and Little Mushroom went out for their walks.

Soon the days began to be a little cooler; and after Chin Ling had lived in the little house with the Liu family for about a month, he was sure they were very poor indeed.

"Little Mushroom," said Mrs. Liu one morning, "I am going out again now to look for work. Today I *must* find something as there is no more money left in the oil jar. If only we could eat the Hairy Bean as Chin Ling does; then it would be easy to find food!"

Mrs. Liu put on her long coat, gave Little Mushroom a good-by pat on his cheek, and went out the little red gate into the street.

Little Mushroom walked over to Chin Ling's cage and looked sadly in at him.

"Chin Ling," he sighed, "what can we do? If only I could make some money so that I could help my mother! But I am too little. No one would give *me* work."

Just at that moment his best friend, Chang San, came running into the little courtyard.

"Little Mushroom!" he cried excitedly. "Guess what I just heard down at the teashop on the corner! A man there says they are holding the great cricket matches today at the Dong An Square. He said that anyone who owns a cricket may enter him, and there will be wonderful prizes. Why don't we take Chin Ling down and try for a prize?"

Little Mushroom could hardly believe his ears. Why, if he should enter Chin Ling in the fights, and if he *did* win a prize, then they would be rich and his mother would not have to worry any more!

"Oh yes, Chang San," cried Little Mushroom, "that is a wonderful idea! Let's go in and tell Chin Ling about it!"

When Chin Ling heard the two little boys talking he felt very worried, as he had not forgotten the days when he had been a weak fighter and the big black cricket had beaten him so many times at wrestling. How could *he* win a fight? But, all the same, he knew that he would fight anything — even an animal as big as a *mouse* — if it would help Little Mushroom and his mother.

Little Mushroom ran to get his long coat and, taking Chin Ling's cage in his hand, ran out into the little street where Chang San was waiting.

Together they walked for a long time, through the crowded streets and under the painted gateways, until at last they came to the Dong An Square, where the cricket fights were to be held.

Little Mushroom looked up at the great buildings and the large, richly dressed men standing about, and his heart quaked inside his little coat. But he remembered his mother and how important it was for Chin Ling to win a prize; so he pushed his way in, motioning to Chang San to follow.

They found the right room for weighing in, and
Chin Ling was put on the scales so that he could be
matched with a cricket of equal weight.

It was not yet time for the matches to begin, so the
two boys wandered around watching the crowd.

Suddenly Chang San pulled Little Mushroom's
sleeve and cried excitedly, "Look over here, Little
Mushroom! The Grand Prize is being shown in a glass
case!"

They ran over to the stand and, sure enough, there
was the most beautiful cricket cage they had ever seen. It
was decorated with a dragon flying through clouds, and
its ivory top was set with precious stones that flashed in
the sunshine.

A white-haired lady in a beautiful gown of deep blue passed by just then and said, "That is the prize offered by the Mayor of the city. The champion of all the matches will win this gourd cage as well as the hundred-dollar prize. Have you a fighter to enter in the matches, lad?"

"Yes, lao tai tai," replied Little Mushroom politely. "He is right here in this cage. He has not fought before; but he is not afraid to try, as we are very poor and need the money to buy our rice."

"I will wish you luck then, my child," smiled the old lady, "and I hope your brave little cricket will win."

At that moment a man went through the crowds shouting that the fights were about to begin, and all the crickets were brought to the rings. Small jars were set upon silk-covered tables, and the people crowded around to watch.

Chin Ling was feeling very nervous as Little Mushroom took him out of his cage for his first fight.

But Little Mushroom said, "Chin Ling, I know you can win; for you are big and strong now."

Feeling brave again, Chin Ling puffed out his chest and started right in to wrestle with the other cricket.

He wrestled as hard as he knew how, and he did so well that the other cricket soon cried out, "You are too strong for me. I give up!"

So Chin Ling won his first match! He was weighed again, and for the next fight he was matched against a cricket who had just won *his* first fight too.

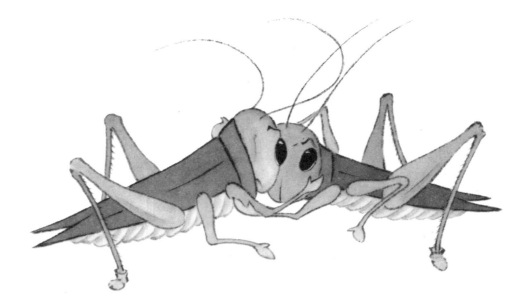

Chin Ling had to wrestle much harder this time. This new cricket was a better wrestler than the other one, and it was not easy to beat him. But finally Chin Ling threw the other cricket and won this match also.

He wrestled again and again, resting between matches. Although he was now almost too tired to move, he was feeling very happy that he had won so far. And he could hear people calling to one another to come and see this unknown cricket who was so brave.

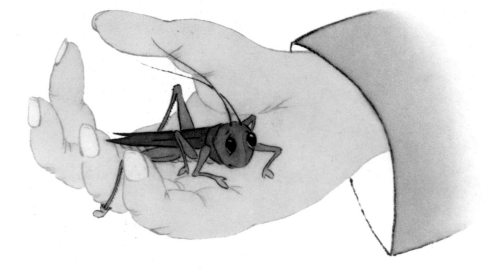

Little Mushroom was almost bursting with pride; but he was modest about his little champion, for, like all Chinese children, he was very polite.

By this time Chin Ling had fought ten battles, and he and another cricket were the only ones left to try for the Grand Prize.

Little Mushroom picked Chin Ling up to put him in his cage for a good rest before the last fight. But, as he did so, he saw that one of his back legs was hanging limply.

"Oh, Chin Ling," he wailed, "your leg has been hurt! What shall we do? You cannot fight with a bad leg!"

Chang San hurried over to see, and gently felt the leg.

"I don't think it is broken," he said slowly. "Only twisted. At any rate we shall have to put him in the ring, whether he can fight or not. But I am afraid there is no hope of winning the Grand Prize now, Little Mushroom. Have you seen the other cricket? He is a big black one and looks very fierce."

Little Mushroom's heart sank; but at that moment the big cricket was brought over by his owner, a large, nice-looking man. There was nothing for Little Mushroom to do but bow politely, and the large man bowed back again.

Chin Ling watched anxiously as his opponent came near. He could hardly believe his eyes when he saw that it was the big cricket who used to fight him in the fields at home. His little heart sank; for, although he had won all his other matches, this was the one cricket in all the world that he knew he could never beat.

The big black cricket looked at Chin Ling in surprise and cried, "You! Why, *you* can't be the cricket I am to fight! How did a weak little thing like you win those other matches? Ha! Ha! Ha! This will be easy."

When Chin Ling heard the big cricket talk like this, he felt himself getting very mad. He decided then and there that he would fight this proud old cricket in spite of his bad leg, no matter what happened.

But when they were put in the ring, Chin Ling began to feel that it was no use. This time he really could not win. He was *so* tired! And his leg was hurting badly too, as he had to drag it around after him.

They wrestled this way and that, with poor Chin Ling fast losing ground. Then, quite suddenly, the black cricket bit him on the shoulder! This was against the rules and it made Chin Ling so angry that he jumped fiercely at the other cricket, knocking him off balance.

Then, to his great surprise, the judges stopped the fight! Little Mushroom quickly picked Chin Ling up and held him carefully in his hands as they all waited to see what the judges would do. They talked in low tones for a while, stroking their long beards.

Then, coming over to Little Mushroom, they said, "We have decided in favor of your cricket, lad. The other cricket did not seem to know the rules of fair play, and yours has shown a fine spirit. He is the new champion."

There was a gasp from the crowd, and then loud cheering for the champion.

Little Mushroom cried, "Oh, Chin Ling! You are the bravest cricket in all Beijing, and you have saved my mother and me. Now we will never be poor again!"

The owner of the big black cricket, whose name was Mr. Tai, heard Little Mushroom and said, "What is this? Are you poor, lad? You have a very fine cricket, and I will buy him for fifty dollars if you will sell him."

Little Mushroom was amazed to hear this, but he knew he could never sell Chin Ling.

So he bowed and said, "Sir, you are a very kind man. But I cannot sell my champion, for he is also my friend."

"A very good answer, my boy," cried Mr. Tai. "But I have another idea. Would you like to take a job in my house and be my Keeper of Crickets?"

At this Little Mushroom wanted to leap for joy, but he managed to reply calmly, "Why, that is very generous of you, sir. I would like it very much. But my mother is in need of work, and if you will take her into your house as a seamstress — see, she has made Chin Ling's hat — then I will be very pleased to become your Keeper of Crickets."

The big man looked astonished at this small boy who knew how to drive such a bargain.

Then he laughed, "All right, my boy! It is settled. But where is your mother now? She should be here to see her son receive the Grand Prize."

Little Mushroom told him that she had been out looking for work but would probably be at home now, as it was almost suppertime.

And at once this jolly man sent off his own ricksha puller to bring Mrs. Liu to the square.

You can imagine Mrs. Liu's surprise at finding that her son was the owner of a champion. She was very proud.

As soon as she arrived, the ceremony began. Little Mushroom was brought to the front of the crowd while the Mayor made a speech about the new champion, Liu Fu. Then he presented Little Mushroom with a large gold-paper envelope, which held the prize money. Next he took down the beautiful gourd cage and handed it to the proud little boy, who turned and gave it to his mother to hold.

Little Mushroom bowed to the Mayor and thanked him in his most grown-up manner.

Then Little Mushroom's new friend, Mr. Tai, said, "Lad, you must be tired and hungry. Come, I will take you to my house for some supper; and then you can go home to bed. Tomorrow you start work as my Keeper of Crickets."

So Little Mushroom, his mother, and Chin Ling live very happily in their little house, going to work each day at Mr. Tai's and coming home to a nice hot supper at night.

And little Chin Ling sits in the sun and remembers the day he became a cricket champion.

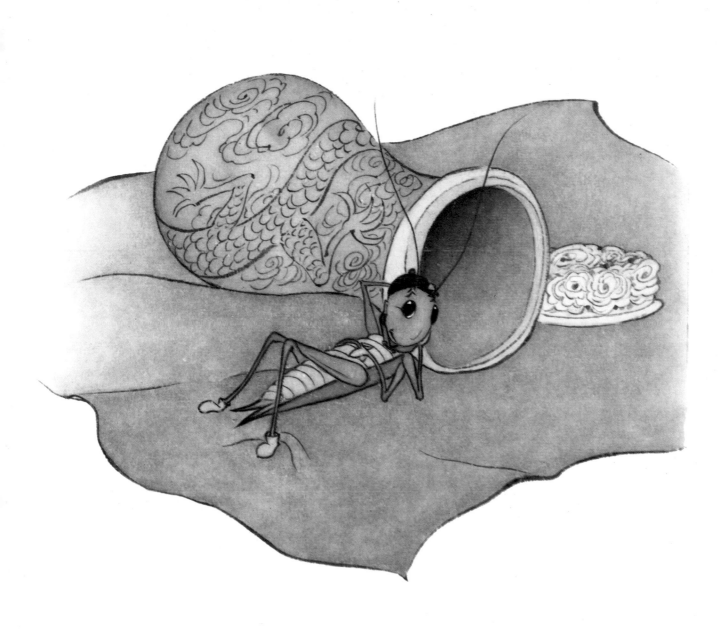